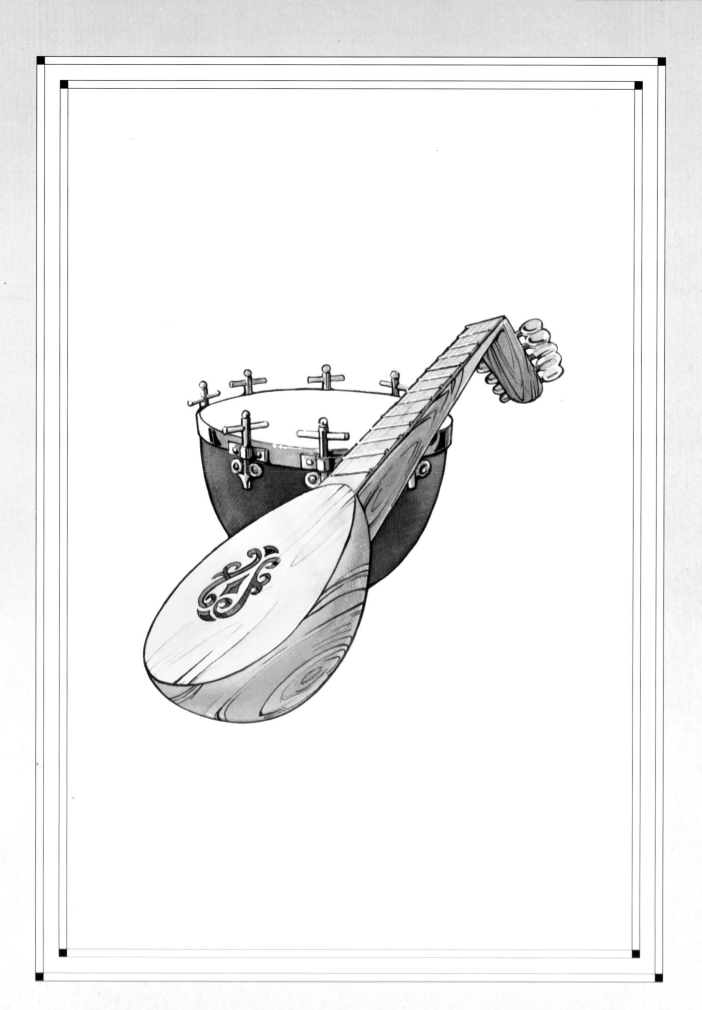

THE BREMEN TOWN MUSICIANS

Illustrated by
Joe Boddy

As Told By
Eugene Evans

The Unicorn Publishing House
New Jersey

There was once a farmer who had a Donkey who had pulled his plow and carried his crops to market for many a long year. The Donkey had been a faithful friend to the farmer, but now his strength was at last gone, and he could neither till the fields nor bear the burden of a heavy cart. The farmer, seeing that the Donkey could no longer help him, began having thoughts that the old fellow's days were coming to an end. The Donkey, however, had other ideas. Frightened of what the farmer might do with him, the Donkey rose early one morning, deciding he would run far away, and set out along the road to Bremen.

"At least there I will be safe," he thought, "and I can become a town-musician to earn my keep."

After running for some time he came upon a large Hound lying by the side of the road. The poor fellow was gasping and wheezing so, that the Donkey thought he might be near death.

"Say, big fellow, are you in need of help? Are you hurt?" asked the Donkey.

"No," replied the Hound, "I'm just worn out from running. You see, I've grown so old and weak I can no longer join the hunt with my master, and he didn't want to take care of me, so he thought he would put me to death. I ran away to save my life, but now I don't know what I'm going to do." And big tears welled up in the old Hound's eyes at the thought of being alone and uncared for.

"Now, now, old chum," said the Donkey kindly, "don't be like that. Why don't you join up with me and come to Bremen. I'm going to be a town-musician and I have need for another to share in the music. I will play the lute and you can beat the kettledrums. What say you, my friend?" The Hound's eyes soon brightened, and he was happy to have a new found friend, so together they set off down the road.

Along the way they happened upon a Cat, who sat right in the middle of the road, her head hung low as she heaved a deep sigh. When they approached, she lifted her big sad eyes up to them, but said nothing.

"What's this rainy day face, Miss Cat?" asked the Donkey. "Have you lost your way?"

"I haven't a way left to lose, Gray-horse," answered the Cat. "I have grown old and tired. My teeth are worn down and my paws ache. My mistress wanted me to chase mice, but I'd rather sit by the fireplace to keep the chill off. She decided to drown me, so I ran away, and now I have nowhere to go. I don't know what will become of me." And the Cat slowly hung her head back down and moaned softly.

"Hey now, come with us to Bremen," begged the Donkey, and the Hound nodded in agreement. "You have sung on many a moonlit night, and would make a fine town-musician."

"Do you think so? I'm not sure—but, yes . . . yes! I'd like to go!" mewed the Cat, and after she had a quick stretch, the three went down the road toward Bremen.

The three soon came to a farmyard where they found a Cock sitting on a gate and crowing with all his might. They could tell that the Cock's crows were not sounds of joy, and his tired and haggard eyes showed that he must be very unhappy.

"Why do you carry on so, Mr. Cock? Morning is long past and there is no need to wake your masters," said the Donkey. "I'll admit, though, if you keep crowing so loud, you could very well wake the dead."

"Well, if I wake the dead, it will be for them to come and take me with them," replied the Cock mournfully.

"Why do you talk like that, friend?" asked the Donkey with concern. "You might be up in your years, but you look like a spry enough fellow."

"The holiday approaches and my Lady will have grand guests coming on Sunday. They will be needing a meal and I am to be it!" answered the Cock in despair. "The mistress will have no pity on her poor servant, and has told the cook to make a fine soup out of me for the morrow. He is going to cut off my head this very evening, so I'm going to crow with a full throat just as long as I can."

"Oh no! We can't let that happen, Red-comb," replied the Donkey; "rather come with us. We are off for Bremen. There is always a better place than where death dwells. We need a voice like yours, as we are going to be town-musicians, so come make music with us!"

The Cock saw the wisdom in this, and quickly agreed. Together the four traveled on toward Bremen.

They followed the road all day until night began to fall, and, knowing that they would not reach Bremen before dark, they decided to rest for the night in the forest. The Donkey and the Hound both found comfortable spots beneath a large oak tree, while the Cat and the Cock climbed up in the tree for greater safety. The Cock being the smallest and most vulnerable of the four, decided to fly all the way to the top branches, where he might have a better look around.

From the top of the great oak he could see throughout the forest. Off in the distance, a very short distance really, the Cock saw a spark of light. After looking long and hard, he made out the shape of a house nestled in the woodland. A soft, inviting glow issued through the windowpanes. The Cock called down to his companions and told them of his discovery. They all agreed that a warm, snug house was far better than the chilly woods.

"These woods could get very cold this night," the Donkey said, "and, besides, we have yet to have our supper."

"Oh, yes indeed!" the Hound added, drooling just a bit; "I would dearly love a couple of bones with some meat on them. Oh, yes, yes, that would be most acceptable!"

So they followed the direction the Cock pointed to until they came to a small, well-lit cottage. What they didn't know, however, was that this was a robbers' hideout. The four came slowly and quietly up to one of the windows. The Hound knew immediately that what he desired lay within, for he could smell the sweet aroma of fresh cooked food, and he smacked his lips with delight. The Donkey, being the biggest, went to the glass and peered in.

"What do you see, Gray-horse?" asked the Cock.

"A great deal, my friend, a great deal," replied the Donkey. "There is a table laid out with all sorts of savory meats, delicious vegetables, and plenty of drink. But there are also three men, robbers to be sure, that are sitting around the table enjoying the feast." And the Donkey watched as the robbers joked with each other, drinking large mugs of ale and comfortably smoking their pipes. He knew these were not men who would afford the least bit of kindness to other men, let alone four homeless animals.

"What shall we do?" asked the Cat.

"Whatever we do, let's be quick about it," the Hound said, "for my stomach is in need of a meaty morsel or two."

The four huddled close together to take counsel on how they might drive away the robbers, and at last they thought of a plan. The Donkey took the lead and set his forefeet on the window ledge. Then the Hound climbed up on his back, followed by the Cat, who rested herself on the Hound's shoulders, and last but not least, the Cock perched softly on the Cat's head. This being done, at a given signal they joined together in song (loud enough to bring down any house); the Donkey brayed, the Hound howled, the Cat mewed, and the Cock crew!

The unlikely chorus went something like this:

"HEHAWWWWWW!"
"AH-HOOOOO!"
"MEOWWWWWW!"
"COCK-A-DOODLE-DOOOOO!"

And right in the middle of their thundering performance, they burst through the windowpane and into the room. The shattering glass and unearthly sounds sent the robbers flying, believing some dark fiend or spirit of the night was upon them! The robbers made for the door, and after fighting to see who would get out first, the three fled screaming into the forest.

As soon as the robbers had gone the four musicians sat down to feast. And what a feast they had! Why, you would think they hadn't eaten for weeks! There were long links of sausage and big meaty bones, chick peas with cabbage, and gallons of ale and sweet wine.

When the four minstrels had finished eating, they decided it was time for bed, and all found places to sleep that suited their tastes. The Donkey took the bed, as it was made of straw, and much like the berth he had known back at the farm. The Hound had always slept behind the door, in case an intruder might enter, and this is where he took his rest. The Cat knew her heart's desire, and curled up on the hearth to be near the warm ashes, while the Cock flew straight up to the roof and perched on a beam for his good-night sleep. And it wasn't long, as they were weary from their long travels, before they all fell into a deep, peaceful sleep.

After midnight the robbers crept silently back toward the cottage. Seeing that there was no longer a light burning in the window, and everything was very quiet, they wondered why they had been so frightened. The leader of the band said, "Perhaps the evil thing has left, or we could have been tricked by some other rogue." And he told one of his men to go down and see if everything was clear. Trembling, the poor fellow did as he was told.

The robber entered the cottage slowly, and, finding all was still and dark, he went to the fireplace to strike a match. But he mistook the glowing eyes of the Cat for live coals from the fire, and tried to light the match by sticking it in her face. Well, she didn't care for this a bit, and flew up in a fury into his face, spitting and scratching, which frightened him so terribly that he made straight for the door. There the Hound was waiting for him, and as the robber tried to pass, the Hound sprang up from behind the door and bit his leg. The robber screamed in terror and fell back, only to be given a powerful kick in the bottom by the Donkey. Ah, but this was not all, for the Cock, awakened by the ruckus, flew wildly about the robber's head and cried, "Cock-a-doodle-doo, cock-a-doodle-doo!" The robber at last found the door and ran, howling in terror, back to his friends.

When he had rejoined the other robbers and caught his breath, he said, "Oh, my friends, what horrors I have beheld! There dwells a terrible witch in the house, who spat fire at me and scratched my face with long, sharp nails. And as I fought her off to reach the door, a man was standing there with a knife, and he stabbed me in the leg. Then from behind, a big black monster attacked me, beating me with a great wooden club. And all this time, as I fled for my life, there was a judge upon the roof, who called out to them, 'Bring the rogue up, do!' So I fought my way to the door and ran as fast as I could. Oh, mercy!"

Never again did the robbers dare to go near the house; but as for the four town-musicians of Bremen, their new home suited them just fine. The four old friends loved their home so much that they never left it. Instead, they passed their days making merry music and loving each and every moment of their wonderful lives together.

And believe me, the mouth of him who last told this story is still warm.

For over a decade, Unicorn has been publishing
richly illustrated editions of classic and contemporary
works for children and adults. To continue this tradition,
WE WOULD LIKE TO KNOW WHAT YOU THINK.

If you would like to send us your suggestions or obtain
a list of our current titles, please write to:
THE UNICORN PUBLISHING HOUSE, INC.
P.O.Box 377
Morris Plains, NJ   07950
ATT: Dept CLP

Printing History 15 14 13 12 11 10 9 8 7 6 5 4 3 2 1

Library of Congress Cataloging-in-Publication Data

Evans, Eugene, 1959-
    The Bremen Town-musicians / illustrated by Joe Boddy; as told by Eugene Evans.
    p. cm.
    An English adaptation of Bremer Stadtmusikanten.
    Summary: Mistreated by their masters, four animal friends set out to become
    musicians in the town of Bremen and encounter a den of thieves.
    ISBN 0-88101-102-9
    [1. Fairy tales. 2. Folklore—Germany.] I. Boddy, Joe, ill.
    II. Bremer Stadtmusikanten. English.   III. Title.
    PZ8.E925Br 1990   90-10974
    398.24'52'0943—dc20   CIP
    [E]   AC